DATE DUE

A COUPLE OF KOOKS

A Richard Jackson Book

Also by Cynthia Rylant

PICTURE BOOKS
Mr. Griggs' Work
All I See
Birthday Presents
Night in the Country
The Relatives Came
This Year's Garden
Miss Maggie
When I Was Young in the Mountains

"THE HENRY AND MUDGE BOOKS"

STORIES
Children of Christmas
Every Living Thing

POETRY
Soda Jerk
Waiting to Waltz: A Childhood

NOVELS
A Kindness
A Fine White Dust
A Blue-Eyed Daisy

AUTOBIOGRAPHY
But I'll Be Back Again

A
COUPLE
OF
KOOKS

and Other Stories
about Love by

Cynthia Rylant

ORCHARD BOOKS   *New York*

TO THRITY

RYL

Orchard Books
A division of Franklin Watts, Inc.
387 Park Avenue South
New York, NY 10016

Quotations from Bill Griffith, *Zippy Stories* (San Francisco: Last Gasp,
1981), reprinted by permission of Bill Griffith.

"Kooks" (David Bowie) © 1971 Bewlay Bros. Music / Fleur Music /
Moth Music Rights for Bewlay Bros. Music and Fleur Music
controlled and administered by Screen Gems-Emi Music, Inc. Rights
for Moth Music controlled and administered by Chrysallis Music. All
Rights Reserved. International Copyright Secured. Used by
Permission.

Manufactured in the United States of America
Book design by Mina Greenstein
The text of this book is set in 14 pt. Perpetua.
10   9   8   7   6   5   4   3   2   1

Library of Congress Cataloging-in-Publication Data
Rylant, Cynthia.
A. couple of kooks and other stories about love.
p.   cm.   Summary: A collection of eight short stories in which
a variety of special characters experience the transfiguring power
of love.
ISBN 0-531-05900-6.   ISBN 0-531-08500-7 (lib. bdg.)
1. Love—Juvenile fiction.   2. Short stories, American.   [1. Love—
Fiction.   2. Short stories.]   I. Title.   PZ7.R982Co   1990
[Fic]—dc20   90-30646   CIP   AC

Contents

A Crush

WHEN the windows of Stan's Hardware started filling up with flowers, everyone in town knew something had happened. Excess flowers usually mean death, but since these were all real flowers bearing the aroma of nature instead of floral preservative, and since they stood bunched in clear mason jars instead of impaled on styrofoam crosses, everyone knew nobody had died. So they all figured somebody had a crush and kept quiet.

There wasn't really a Stan of Stan's Hardware. Dick Wilcox was the owner, and since he'd never liked his own name, he gave his store half the name of his childhood hero, Stan Laurel in the movies. Dick had been married for twenty-seven years. Once, his wife

Helen had dropped a German chocolate cake on his head at a Lion's Club dance, so Dick and Helen were not likely candidates for the honest expression of the flowers in those clear mason jars lining the windows of Stan's Hardware, and speculation had to move on to Dolores.

Dolores was the assistant manager at Stan's and had worked there for twenty years, since high school. She knew the store like a mother knows her baby, so Dick—who had trouble keeping up with things like prices and new brands of drywall compound—tried to keep himself busy in the back and give Dolores the run of the floor. This worked fine because the carpenters and plumbers and painters in town trusted Dolores and took her advice to heart. They also liked her tattoo.

Dolores was the only woman in town with a tattoo. On the days she went sleeveless, one could see it on the taut brown skin of her upper arm: "Howl at the Moon." The picture was of a baying coyote which must have been a dark gray in its early days but which had faded to the color of the spackling paste Dolores stocked in the third aisle. Nobody had gotten out of Dolores the true story behind the tattoo. Some of the men who came in liked to show off their own, and they'd roll up their sleeves or pull open their shirts, exhibiting bald eagles and rattlesnakes and Confederate flags, and they'd try to coax out of Dolores the history of her coyote. All of the men had gotten their tattoos when they were in the service, drunk on weekend leave and full of the spitfire of young soldiers. Dolores had never been in the service and she'd never seen weekend leave and there wasn't a tattoo parlor anywhere near. They couldn't figure why or where any half-sober woman would have a howling coyote ground into the soft skin of her upper arm. But Dolores wasn't telling.

That the flowers in Stan's front window had anything to do with Dolores seemed completely improbable. As far as anyone knew, Dolores had never been in love nor had anyone ever been in love with her. Some believed it was the tattoo, of course, or the fine dark hair coating Dolores's upper lip which kept suitors away. Some felt it was because Dolores was just more of a man than most of the men in town, and fellows couldn't figure out how to court someone who knew more about the carburetor of a car or the back side of a washing machine than they did. Others thought Dolores simply didn't want love. This was a popular theory among the women in town who sold Avon and Mary Kay cosmetics. Whenever one of them ran into the hardware for a package of light bulbs or some batteries, she would mentally pluck every one of the black hairs above Dolores's lip. Then she'd wash that grease out of Dolores's hair, give her a good blunt cut, dress her in a decent silk-blend blouse with a nice Liz Claiborne skirt from the Sports line, and, finally, tone down that swarthy, longshoreman look of Dolores's with a concealing beige foundation, some frosted peach lipstick, and a good gray liner for the eyes.

Dolores simply didn't want love, the Avon lady would think as she walked back to her car carrying her little bag of batteries. If she did, she'd fix herself up.

The man who was in love with Dolores and who brought her zinnias and cornflowers and nasturtiums and marigolds and asters and four o'clocks in clear mason jars did not know any of this. He did not know that men showed Dolores their tattoos. He did not know that Dolores understood how to use and to sell a belt sander. He did not know that Dolores needed some concealing beige foundation so she could get someone to love her. The man who brought flowers to Dolores on Wednesdays when the hardware opened its doors at 7:00 a.m. didn't care who Dolores had ever been or what anyone had ever thought of her. He loved her and he wanted to bring her flowers.

Ernie had lived in this town all of his life and had never before met Dolores. He was thirty-three years old, and for thirty-one of those years he had lived at home with his mother in a small, dark house on the edge of town near Beckwith's Orchards. Ernie had been a beautiful baby, with a shock of shining black hair and large blue eyes and a round, wise face. But as he had grown, it had become clearer and clearer that though he was indeed a perfectly beautiful child, his mind had not developed with the same perfection. Ernie would not be able to speak in sentences until he was six years old. He would not be able to count the apples in a bowl until he was eight. By the time he was ten, he could sing a simple song. At age twelve, he understood what a joke was. And when he was twenty, something he saw on television made him cry.

Ernie's mother kept him in the house with her because it was easier, so Ernie knew nothing of the world except this house. They lived, the two of them, in tiny dark rooms always illuminated by the glow of a television set, Ernie's bags of Oreos and Nutter Butters littering the floor, his baseball cards scattered across the sofa, his heavy winter coat thrown over the arm of a chair so he could wear it whenever he wanted, and his box of Burpee seed packages sitting in the middle of the kitchen table.

These Ernie cherished. The seeds had been delivered to his home by mistake. One day a woman wearing a brown uniform had pulled up in a brown truck, walked quickly to the front porch of Ernie's house, set a box down, and with a couple of toots of her horn, driven off again. Ernie had watched her through the curtains, and when she was gone, had ventured onto the porch and shyly, cautiously, picked up the box. His mother checked it when he carried it inside. The box didn't have their name on it but the brown truck was gone, so whatever was in the box was theirs to keep. Ernie pulled off the heavy tape, his fingers trembling, and found inside the box more little packages of seeds than he could count. He lifted them out, one by one, and examined the beautiful photographs of flowers on each. His mother was not interested, had returned to the television, but Ernie sat down at the kitchen table and quietly looked at each package for a long time, his fingers running across the slick paper and outlining the shapes of zinnias and cornflowers and nasturtiums and marigolds and asters and four o'clocks, his eyes drawing up their colors.

Two months later Ernie's mother died. A neighbor found her at the mailbox beside the road. People from the county courthouse came out to get Ernie, and as they ushered him from the home he would never see again, he picked up the box of seed packages from his kitchen table and passed through the doorway.

Eventually Ernie was moved to a large white house near the main street of town. This house was called a group home, because in it lived a group of people who, like Ernie, could not live on their own. There were six of them. Each had his own room. When Ernie was shown the room that would be his, he put the box of Burpee seeds—which he had kept with him since his mother's death—on the little table beside the bed and then he sat down on the bed and cried.

Ernie cried every day for nearly a month. And then he stopped. He dried his tears and he learned how to bake refrigerator biscuits and how to dust mop and what to do if the indoor plants looked brown.

Ernie loved watering the indoor plants and it was this pleasure which finally drew him outside. One of the young men who worked at the group home—a college student named Jack—grew a large garden in the back of the house. It was full of tomato vines and the large yellow blossoms of healthy squash. During his first summer at the house, Ernie would stand at the kitchen window, watching Jack and sometimes a resident of the home move among the vegetables. Ernie was curious, but too afraid to go into the garden.

Then one day when Ernie was watching through the window, he noticed that Jack was ripping open several slick little packages and emptying them into the ground. Ernie panicked and ran to his room. But the box of Burpee seeds was still there on his table, untouched. He grabbed it, slid it under his bed, then went back through the house and out into the garden as if he had done this every day of his life.

He stood beside Jack, watching him empty seed packages into the soft black soil, and as the packages were emptied, Ernie asked for them, holding out his hand, his eyes on the photographs of red radishes and purple eggplant. Jack handed the empty packages over with a smile and with that gesture became Ernie's first friend.

Jack tried to explain to Ernie that the seeds would grow into vegetables but Ernie could not believe this until he saw it come true. And when it did, he looked all the more intently at the packages of zinnias and cornflowers and the rest hidden beneath his bed. He thought more deeply about them but he could not carry them to the garden. He could not let the garden have his seeds.

That was the first year in the large white house.

The second year, Ernie saw Dolores, and after that he thought of nothing else but her and of the photographs of flowers beneath his bed.

Jack had decided to take Ernie downtown for breakfast every Wednesday morning to ease him into the world outside that of the group home. They left very early, at 5:45 a.m., so there would be few people and almost no traffic to frighten Ernie and make him beg for his room. Jack and Ernie drove to the Big Boy restaurant which sat across the street from Stan's Hardware. There they ate eggs and bacon and French toast among those whose work demanded rising before the sun: bus drivers, policemen, nurses, mill workers. Their first time in the Big Boy, Ernie was too nervous to eat. The second time, he could eat but he couldn't look up. The third time, he not only ate everything on his plate, but he lifted his head and he looked out the window of the Big Boy restaurant toward Stan's Hardware across the street. There he saw a dark-haired woman in jeans and a black T-shirt unlocking the front door of the building, and that was the moment Ernie started loving Dolores and thinking about giving up his seeds to the soft black soil of Jack's garden.

Love is such a mystery, and when it strikes the heart of one as mysterious as Ernie himself, it can hardly be spoken of. Ernie could not explain to Jack why he went directly to his room later that morning, pulled the box of Burpee seeds from under his bed, then grabbed Jack's hand in the kitchen and walked with him to the garden where Ernie had come to believe things would grow. Ernie handed the packets of seeds one by one to Jack, who stood in silent admiration of the lovely photographs before asking Ernie several

times, "Are you sure you want to plant these?" Ernie
was sure. It didn't take him very long, and when the
seeds all lay under the moist black earth, Ernie carried
his empty packages inside the house and spent the rest
of the day spreading them across his bed in different
arrangements.

That was in June. For the next several Wednesdays
at 7:00 a.m. Ernie watched every movement of the
dark-haired woman behind the lighted windows of
Stan's Hardware. Jack watched Ernie watch Dolores,
and discreetly said nothing.

When Ernie's flowers began growing in July, Ernie
spent most of his time in the garden. He would watch
the garden for hours, as if he expected it suddenly to
move or to impress him with a quick trick. The fragile
green stems of his flowers stood uncertainly in the soil,
like baby colts on their first legs, but the young plants
performed no magic for Ernie's eyes. They saved their
shows for the middle of the night and next day surprised Ernie with tender small blooms in all the colors
the photographs had promised.

The flowers grew fast and hardy, and one early Wednesday morning when they looked as big and bright as their pictures on the empty packages, Ernie pulled a glass canning jar off a dusty shelf in the basement of his house. He washed the jar, half filled it with water, then carried it to the garden where he placed in it one of every kind of flower he had grown. He met Jack at the car and rode off to the Big Boy with the jar of flowers held tight between his small hands. Jack told him it was a beautiful bouquet.

When they reached the door of the Big Boy, Ernie stopped and pulled at Jack's arm, pointing to the building across the street. "OK," Jack said, and he led Ernie to the front door of Stan's Hardware. It was 6:00 a.m. and the building was still dark. Ernie set the clear mason jar full of flowers under the sign that read "Closed," then he smiled at Jack and followed him back across the street to get breakfast.

When Dolores arrived at seven and picked up the jar of zinnias and cornflowers and nasturtiums and marigolds and asters and four o'clocks, Ernie and Jack were watching her from a booth in the Big Boy. Each had a wide smile on his face as Dolores put her nose to the flowers. Ernie giggled. They watched the lights of the hardware store come up and saw Dolores place the clear mason jar on the ledge of the front window. They drove home still smiling.

All the rest of that summer Ernie left a jar of flowers every Wednesday morning at the front door of Stan's Hardware. Neither Dick Wilcox nor Dolores could figure out why the flowers kept coming, and each of them assumed somebody had a crush on the other. But the flowers had an effect on them anyway. Dick started spending more time out on the floor making conversation with the customers, while Dolores stopped wearing T-shirts to work and instead wore crisp white blouses with the sleeves rolled back off her wrists. Occasionally she put on a bracelet.

By summer's end Jack and Ernie had become very good friends, and when the flowers in the garden behind their house began to wither, and Ernie's face began to grow gray as he watched them, Jack brought home

one bright day in late September a great long box.
Ernie followed Jack as he carried it down to the basement and watched as Jack pulled a long glass tube
from the box and attached this tube to the wall above
a table. When Jack plugged in the tube's electric cord,
a soft lavender light washed the room.

"Sunshine," said Jack.

Then he went back to his car for a smaller box. He
carried this down to the basement where Ernie still
stood staring at the strange light. Jack handed Ernie
the small box, and when Ernie opened it he found
more little packages of seeds than he could count, with
new kinds of photographs on the slick paper.

"Violets," Jack said, pointing to one of them.

Then he and Ernie went outside to get some dirt.

Checkouts

HER PARENTS had moved her to Cincinnati, to a large house with beveled glass windows and several porches and the *history* her mother liked to emphasize. You'll love the house, they said. You'll be lonely at first, they admitted, but you're so nice you'll make friends fast. And as an impulse tore at her to lie on the floor, to hold to their ankles and tell them she felt she was dying, to offer anything, anything at all, so they might allow her to finish growing up in the town of her childhood, they firmed their mouths and spoke from their chests and they said, It's decided.

They moved her to Cincinnati, where for a month she spent the greater part of every day in a room full of beveled glass windows, sifting through photographs of the life she'd lived and left behind. But it is difficult work, suffering, and in its own way a kind of art, and finally she didn't have the energy for it anymore, so she emerged from the beautiful house and fell in love with a bag boy at the supermarket. Of course, this didn't happen all at once, just like that, but in the sequence of things that's exactly the way it happened.

She liked to grocery shop. She loved it in the way some people love to drive long country roads, because doing it she could think and relax and wander. Her parents wrote up the list and handed it to her and off she went without complaint to perform what they regarded as a great sacrifice of her time and a sign that she was indeed a very nice girl. She had never told them how much she loved grocery shopping, only that she was "willing" to do it. She had an intuition which told her that her parents were not safe for sharing such strong, important facts about herself. Let them think they knew her.

Once inside the supermarket, her hands firmly around the handle of the cart, she would lapse into a kind of reverie and wheel toward the produce. Like a Tibetan monk in solitary meditation, she calmed to a point of deep, deep happiness; this feeling came to her, reliably, if strangely, only in the supermarket.

Then one day the bag boy dropped her jar of mayonnaise and that is how she fell in love.

He was nervous—first day on the job—and along had come this fascinating girl, standing in the checkout line with the unfocused stare one often sees in young children, her face turned enough away that he might take several full looks at her as he packed sturdy bags full of food and the goods of modern life. She interested him because her hair was red and thick, and in it she had placed a huge orange bow, nearly the size of a small hat. That was enough to distract him, and when finally it was her groceries he was packing, she looked at him and smiled and he could respond only by busting her jar of mayonnaise on the floor, shards of glass and oozing cream decorating the area around his feet.

She loved him at exactly that moment, and if he'd known this perhaps he wouldn't have fallen into the brown depression he fell into, which lasted the rest of his shift. He believed he must have looked the jackass in her eyes, and he envied the sureness of everyone around him: the cocky cashier at the register, the grim and harried store manager, the bland butcher, and the brazen bag boys who smoked in the warehouse on their breaks. He wanted a second chance. Another chance to be confident and say witty things to her as he threw tin cans into her bags, persuading her to allow him to help her to her car so he might learn just a little about her, check out the floor of the car for signs of hobbies or fetishes and the bumpers for clues as to beliefs and loyalties.

But he busted her jar of mayonnaise and nothing else worked out for the rest of the day.

Strange, how attractive clumsiness can be. She left the supermarket with stars in her eyes, for she had loved the way his long nervous fingers moved from the conveyor belt to the bags, how deftly (until the mayonnaise) they had picked up her items and placed them into her bags. She had loved the way the hair kept falling into his eyes as he leaned over to grab a box or a tin. And the tattered brown shoes he wore with no socks. And the left side of his collar turned in rather than out.

The bag boy seemed a wonderful contrast to the perfectly beautiful house she had been forced to accept as her home, to the *history* she hated, to the loneliness she had become used to, and she couldn't wait to come back for more of his awkwardness and dishevelment.

Incredibly, it was another four weeks before they saw each other again. As fate would have it, her visits to the supermarket never coincided with his schedule to bag. Each time she went to the store, her eyes scanned the checkouts at once, her heart in her mouth. And each hour he worked, the bag boy kept one eye on the door, watching for the red-haired girl with the big orange bow.

Yet in their disappointment these weeks there was a kind of ecstasy. It is reason enough to be alive, the hope you may see again some face which has meant something to you. The anticipation of meeting the bag boy eased the girl's painful transition into her new and jarring life in Cincinnati. It provided for her an anchor amid all that was impersonal and unfamiliar, and she spent less time on thoughts of what she had left behind as she concentrated on what might lie ahead. And for the boy, the long and often tedious hours at the supermarket which provided no challenge other than that of showing up the following workday . . . these hours became possibilities of mystery and romance for him as he watched the electric doors for the girl in the orange bow.

And when finally they did meet up again, neither offered a clue to the other that he, or she, had been the object of obsessive thought for weeks. She spotted him as soon as she came into the store, but she kept her eyes strictly in front of her as she pulled out a cart and wheeled it toward the produce. And he, too, knew the instant she came through the door—though the orange bow was gone, replaced by a small but bright yellow flower instead—and he never once turned his head in her direction but watched her from the corner of his vision as he tried to swallow back the fear in his throat.

It is odd how we sometimes deny ourselves the very pleasure we have longed for and which is finally within our reach. For some perverse reason she would not have been able to articulate, the girl did not bring her cart up to the bag boy's checkout when her shopping was done. And the bag boy let her leave the store, pretending no notice of her.

This is often the way of children, when they truly want a thing, to pretend that they don't. And then they grow angry when no one tries harder to give them this thing they so casually rejected, and they soon find themselves in a rage simply because they cannot say yes when they mean yes. Humans are very complicated. (And perhaps cats, who have been known to react in the same way, though the resulting rage can only be guessed at.)

The girl hated herself for not checking out at the boy's line, and the boy hated himself for not catching her eye and saying hello, and they most sincerely hated each other without having ever exchanged even two minutes of conversation.

Eventually—in fact, within the week—a kind and intelligent boy who lived very near her beautiful house asked the girl to a movie and she gave up her fancy for the bag boy at the supermarket. And the bag boy himself grew so bored with his job that he made a desperate search for something better and ended up in a bookstore where scores of fascinating girls lingered like honeybees about a hive. Some months later the bag boy and the girl with the orange bow again crossed paths, standing in line with their dates at a movie theater, and, glancing toward the other, each smiled slightly, then looked away, as strangers on public buses often do, when one is moving off the bus and the other is moving on.

Certain
Rainbows

GRANDFATHER of the bride. My days of top billing are over, I suppose. Once I was the star of the pageant, the groom in all his splendor. Now here I sit on a warm folding chair holding a party cup of pastel mints in my hand, watching the young ones in tuxedoes and white lace make new the dance I, too, once danced.

Do they have the same thoughts, the same feelings we had when Lois wore her mother's white dress and I borrowed Uncle Tony's black suit and we plunged into real life in the space of an afternoon? And oh yes, it was that fast, and a shock like a dive into Maine water. We were children till then, till the wedding. We had no idea how everything would change, how the world would feel to us absolutely altered the following day, and though our bodies we recognized as our own, and our town and our families and our friends we recognized as those we had known so familiarly before the wedding . . . still we fell out of time and space into something else and we were never, ever able to go back.

Oh dear, I do wax philosophical. Let me drink of this champagne and look at my beautiful granddaughter there in the traditional white, aglow, and give thanks, utterly blessed thanks, that I have lived to see this, have lived to know that life does not ever stop or even change in any substantial way. And thanks that I have been able to ride it awhile.

I remember nearly fifty years ago George and I smoked through three packs of Camels as we lingered in the parking lot of the church, waiting for Lois and the bridesmaids finally to have ready their bouquets and pearl necklaces and roses in the hair for that grand entrance beautiful young women are capable of making. I did not know then that all young women are beautiful, all of them, as I know it now, and if I could I would go back to that church and stop fidgeting in the parking lot and prepare myself instead to look, really look, at the masterpieces Lois and her blushing beauties were. It is not the absence of wrinkles which makes young women so beautiful. Oh no, that there are no lines on their faces is their one and only disadvantage, for it makes them less interesting than people who have lived life. The beauty of young women lies completely in the awe they have of *themselves*. Their reverence for their bodies, their soft hands and arms and shoulders and mouths. Their delight in beautiful colors, the florals and paisleys, the velvets, the taffetas, the silks they are discovering like gold. The beauty of young women rests in their innocent surprise at the ways in which they can be transformed and their shyness in revealing that transformation to others. I was too nervous, too self-absorbed, my wedding day to see this wonder of female nature, and now I must take notice, look with a young man's eyes at my lovely young granddaughter and the pink girls at her side who today have become the lilies they did not know they were.

See poor Esther there. My long-suffering sister-in-law makes it a point to feel bad no matter the occasion, even if the occasion is an outdoor reception on one of the most beautiful April afternoons any of us can remember in a long time, though we are encased in the fragrance of tulips and narcissus, sweet perfume, delicious food, and even the talc of babies' skin. Esther dear, time is fleeting. Will you, on your death bed, mourn the life you never cared to savor because you were too busy counting your losses?

What a way of life. Thank God I knew better, know better now.

I thought I would die a young man. Maybe that is why I celebrated every warm bath, hot cinnamon roll, feather pillow, red geranium, every scent of pine and ginger, every kiss . . . perhaps I took some things for granted but I tried, every day, I truly believe, to revere others. I thought I would die a young man and here I am, seventy-five, drinking champagne. It's lovely.

They believe they are in love, my granddaughter

and her fine new husband. I believe this as well, though all about me I see the faces of doubt, the faces which cannot, for a single afternoon, believe in the possibility of being in love. Instead they murmur among themselves, already placing mean bets on how long the marriage will last. Yes, the boy makes little money. Yes, they are both very young. Yes, there is the problem of religion. But must being in love, in fact even marrying, be a permanent thing in order to be real? How many years will these smug ones require of those two young lovers before they regard them as authentic? A thing which lasts is not always superior to that which is fleeting. How many men have I witnessed stay with the same company twenty, thirty, forty years and gain the respect and admiration of their society for the so-called commitment they have made, while a man who changes careers several times during the course of his life, perhaps making *less* money with each change rather than more, is regarded as unstable, unreliable, immature. Only the old know how long life really is. And knowing this, it is the old who can be willing to let a man live his dreams, though they may take fifty years to find. It is the old who look with disbelief at young men and women who design for themselves a particular way of life and force themselves to hold to it no matter what. It is the old who know the foolery of this, for we know there is time and time and time to try everything, even falling in love, a million ways. Yes, life is short, as they say, but in another sense it is long, long, long.

Those two young people are in love as surely as this is spring, and if their feelings last not another day, for this moment they are as real as anything God Himself ever created. And let's face it—some of God's best beauties are momentary indeed. I have seen certain rainbows . . .

Lois and I believed we would be in love forever. We believed it most fiercely, passionately, reverently. We stayed in love for a very long time, longer than most of our married friends who are together still, and then one day we were not anymore. Lois is no better at pretense than I and would not accept that passionate love was no longer a possibility for her life. We divorced and she met Ed, and the colors alone which she began to wear, the wild earrings, the odd shoes, the strange scarves . . . these alone were proof enough for me that she was indeed in love with Ed and had indeed fallen out of love with me. After enough time had passed to adjust, I looked at her with sheer delight. And do still. Just *look* at that hat she's wearing! Marvelous.

I have not yet met anyone for whom I might wear strange hats or sing imbecilic songs or dance the limbo or completely flip-flop religions. I meet widows, and like them, but I have found to my dismay they seem to prefer the company of women wholly to that of men and are, in fact, leery of us. I can't blame them, of course. Why would they *want* to be someone's wife again? Perhaps I will meet one who would want to be someone's lover instead. Perhaps. It will be difficult. Society has been relentless in grinding down the natural sexual feelings of its women. Of course it would, since society is controlled by men who are terrified women might one day sort through them like cantaloupes at the supermarket, buying only the best.

My granddaughter there. I am so proud she is following her own heart. Therapists may have us believe that our hearts are not reliable beacons to follow, that our passions are not to be trusted if we want to make sane choices for our lives, if we want to live in peace and not chaos. Perhaps so. Peace should always be preferable to chaos I suppose. Perhaps writing out the pros and cons and choosing accordingly is a more intelligent way to live and even to love. They tell us we always have choices, even about loving.

I thought I would die a young man. I didn't. Instead I had the chaos of two unexpected children (in addition to the expected ones). The chaos of a failed business (hot-air ballooning, imagine it!). The chaos of debt (it was an exquisite sailboat, nevertheless). The chaos of divorce (I didn't understand about the colors yet). And still, if one of those lovely women over there, near the violinists, crossed the lawn toward me, pulled this empty chair alongside mine, removed the mints and the champagne from my hands, leaned over in a mist of perfume and whispered in my ear, "I love you," I would follow her, with all my heart and soul, thanking God all the while how long, long, long life can go on.

His
Just Due

HE'D BEEN driving coal trucks all his life and when the mines shut down and there wasn't any more work, he just hung out at the truck stop talking to Zelda and Chuck and buying some old guy a coffee now and then. The last thing he ever expected to find in that place was someone who believed everything he said and wanted to stay.

His name was Boyd and he'd grown up in a family of five, the third child behind two older brothers, and as a result he had always carried a sort of third-place attitude with him. Nobody ever remembers who comes in third, not even in the Olympics, and because Boyd never could change his standing in the race, couldn't go back next year and be born second or even first in the family, he resigned himself to this unfortunate feeling of *almost* having everything, and sure enough life arranged itself to work out this way. He almost went to technical school, he almost won a Chevy Nova, he almost got married, and he almost died when his coal truck rolled over on him. For the fourth thing, he had no complaints. But all the rest of the near misses he regarded as his basic lot in life because he simply never expected to actually get something.

In the truck stop he got something and that is what this story is about.

The truck stop had a meat loaf smell to it, with a hint of pork gravy around its edges, and it reminded him so of Sunday dinners when he was a boy that a certain calm would fall over him the moment he walked through its door. It seemed the place for comfort when the mines and his job went bust.

Zelda, the head waitress, had been serving him 5:00 a.m. coffee for years like a kind of mother, and now when he came in late in the morning or maybe nine or ten of an evening when most working men are in bed, she brought his coffee with two creams to him as a parent might minister to a sick child, with a soft pucker to her lips and an odd little line in her brow, and he didn't mind it, not at all, because really he was scared, more scared than he'd ever been, and he'd reach for the coffee and her face like a lifeline and use these to stay afloat awhile. Sometimes he'd come in too late to catch the grits—they were usually all gone by noon—and Chuck in the kitchen would just read his mind and cook up a little bit only for him, and these, as well, coming hot from the kitchen and passed to him from Zelda's strong hands, helped him breathe easier and laugh a little and relax enough to look around and see who was in the place.

As a boy he'd always been a watcher. The safest he ever felt was in a room full of people who weren't paying him much attention and would not notice if his eyes moved across them, quickly enough to be polite but long enough to get some sense of things. The truck stop was perfect for a watcher and Boyd practically entered an ecstatic trance as he sipped his coffee at one of the little green formica tables and, like the light from a lighthouse, swept his eyes over the other tables, catching the front door in this path, thinking of nothing else in the world but what he saw before him.

What he saw before him one eventful morning was a gold medal, though he didn't at first recognize it as such. What he saw was simply a young woman with a small child, a boy, who sat in one of the blue booster seats Zelda kept near the register for kids who didn't fit high chairs and sank too deep in the regulars. The boy fed himself, applesauce and cottage cheese this day, and the mess of it was all over him, even in his hair, because his young mother forgot to keep wiping him off and instead took small drinks from a glass of milk and stared long out the window toward Highway 14. Her mouth was dry and pale and her eyes held a weariness out of place for one so young and pretty and the mother of such a creative diner. Boyd forgot his politeness, and since she was looking out the window anyway, he stared at her and her baby as one might a glowing hearth or a deer in a clearing or the moon.

Then just as Zelda was crossing the floor with his plate of eggs in her hands, two things happened. The baby started choking and an angry young man came through the truck stop door. A seasoned watcher has peripheral vision that gets wider and wider with time and Boyd saw these two things happening in exactly the same moment and with exactly the same feeling of alarm toward them both. He set down his cup.

The angry young man, whose western boots rang hard on the slick tile floor, strode through the room, brushing against the corners of tables and looking straight at the woman and the child as the latter coughed and gagged and spit wet white curds into the towel his young mother held beneath his chin. "OK, honey, OK," she was saying in her soft voice as the boots reached the table and a hand grasped the back of her neck.

Zelda set down Boyd's eggs just as Boyd scooted back his chair.

All at once the whole story was there. The young man was obviously drunk now and nearly always drunk at home. The young woman had fled with her child. Boyd could see her throwing the baby's things into a shopping bag in the middle of the night while her husband, passed out in a stupor, snored on the living room couch. She stuffed her things into a small suitcase. Her heart pounded as she ran out to the car with the bags and back in for the baby. The child was sleeping and she picked him up gently, noiselessly, letting his lolling head find anchor on her shoulder as she walked quickly past the man she could not trust not to kill her. Tears streaming down her face she backed her car into the road and drove off for anywhere, anyplace. She checked into a motel some miles down the highway under a different name and today she tried to soothe the child who choked on the spoonful of cottage cheese he'd fed himself as the man who loved, not her, but the handiness of having her take care of things while he drank to oblivion, put his hand on the back of her neck.

Everyone in the truck stop now had turned into a watcher. Everyone knew the danger and everyone waited to see it rise, over at the table with the woman and the baby and the angry young man standing above them.

The young man began speaking to her in the loud whispers which are usually reserved for threats, and the young woman tried to draw away from him, tried to pry his fingers from the back of her neck, tried to say the right words to make him sane and sober and safe. But there were no such words, and as the young man grew meaner and the young woman grew smaller and the baby continued to gag, Boyd stood up, walked over to that table, lifted the coughing child with one arm and with the hand of his other arm tightened his fingers to the back of the young man's neck.

Instantly the woman was released and the young man's hands flew up to latch onto Boyd's fingers. What happened next happened so fast that everybody in the restaurant had a different story for it but the end result was the young man driving off in his pickup, one of his boots smashed down hard on the accelerator, and Boyd and Zelda and Chuck from the kitchen taking turns cleaning off the baby and wiping away his mother's tears and bringing out coffee and lollipops and unconsciously committing every part of themselves to this lost mother and boy.

Stories do have happy endings and Boyd would have been the last to believe it, but they do, and the way things worked out was so perfect, so perfect a win across the finish line, that he was even grateful for all of the almosts of his history because he had an even keener, exquisite sense of finally coming in first.

The angry young man left town. Whatever it was Boyd said to him between the door of the truck stop and the door of the pickup was so perfect, so excellently worded, that it worked, instantly and finally, and the young man left town, period. Boyd was never able to remember what he said, what perfect words he'd chosen. He was living on a different plane altogether as he moved and talked his way across that gravel lot, and like a soldier who pulls his buddy through enemy fire but later can't remember how, Boyd could only have faith that the extraordinary had happened and believe he had caused it.

He walked back into the truck stop and went toward the woman he'd watched like a moon and from then on so many extraordinary things happened that he became used to them, and grew to expect them, and finally came to feel that when everything worked it was simply the way of life and his just due for being here.

He took the woman and her baby to his tiny home that day and he cleared all the newspapers off his couch so she might have a decent place to sit and all the history books off the bed in the back room so the boy might have a decent place to nap, and to help her feel happy again he put an old Johnny Rivers tape on and cooked up a pot of hot chocolate with real milk and real cocoa and vanilla and salt and he put bread in the toaster and apple butter on the table and all that afternoon and early into the evening he talked to her; and as the light outside changed, the light on her face changed, too, as if she were drawing all of the fading day into the house for herself, for some hope and some ease.

She slept on the back room bed with her baby that night like a gold medal in the velvet box of the house, and Boyd whistled as he washed up the dirty saucers and cups and scrubbed scalded milk from the sides of the cooking pot.

And his life worked this way: she was hired on as a waitress at the truck stop. She loved her job. She loved the strong hug she got from Zelda every morning and the way Chuck made her take home extra pieces of pie at the end of the day, and the customers who always asked, "How's that boy of yours doing?" Boyd got on with a house-painting crew and discovered he liked being up high and outside and in the company of others. Zelda's sister, who already had a little girl of her own, baby-sat the child, who continued to sleep on Boyd's back bedroom bed while his mother, after a time, moved into the softness of Boyd's own bed. Boyd painted all the rooms of his tiny house white, and in the boy's back bedroom he hung a prism in the window so that just about five o'clock each day as the sun wound its way around that side of the yard, a giant luminescent rainbow painted itself like a halo on the south wall behind the baby's sleeping head, and the whole place sat quiet and perfect and complete.

Do You Know That Feeling?

D<small>EAR</small> M<small>AMA</small>,

Waiting is always the hardest part. He works at the gas station and stops by after work and you know how I always have to have everything ready to go right on the dot? Well, he loves chicken noodle soup from the box and Duncan Hines fudge brownies and nearly every night when he comes by I will have one or the other ready for him and sometimes both. I'll get the soup to boil and then to simmering exactly ten to nine when he's supposed to come at nine. Or I'll put the brownies in at eight-twenty-seven on the dot so they'll have twenty-five minutes to bake and eight minutes exactly to cool for coming out of the pan. And more times than not, he'll be late. I'll try to keep the soup from going all greasy on top and the brownies from getting hard around the edges, but still somewhat warm, and I swear to you, Mama, with a young man waiting is the hardest part.

I never expected to like this boy, Ma. He's just barely tall as I am and has acne something awful. He's got these big acne boils on his back, and when I give him a back scratch, it's like trying to follow a particularly tricky road map, I have to take all these detours and bypasses. That's so he won't get one of those things hooked by my fingernails. His teeth aren't too good either, Mama. One day he came to school with his front lip swollen straight out like the cover of a *National Geographic* because one of his rotten teeth had caused some bad infection in his mouth. I barely recognized him, I swear it, and I got this flash as I looked at him that love is fickle indeed, Mama, because if he had stayed looking like that, there is no way on God's good earth I would have continued going steady with that boy.

But some penicillin in the hind end got his lip back

to normal, and I can live with the zits and a few bad teeth.

I like him, Mama, don't ask me why. Maybe the reason I like him so much is because he likes *me* so much. You wouldn't believe how totally smitten he is with me. Is it possible, do you think, to love somebody just because he's so good at loving *you*, or is that the most conceited thing you ever heard of? He loves my hair, Mama. Says I have the prettiest hair he's ever seen. And the biggest lonesome eyes. But I won't tell you what he says about my legs, to save us both from blushing.

And his own mother is like a mama to me, if it's all right to tell you that. We'll drive over to his house after sixth period (seniors get to skip seventh period if they've got a job), and his house'll be empty and we'll make us some hot instant tea with a teaspoon of sugar and some canned milk and we'll have a piece of apple pie or lemon pound cake from the fridge because we know how happy it makes his mama when we eat up her food. And we'll sit at the kitchen table without turning on any lights in the house even if it's cloudy outside, talking about getting married and buying a trailer first and living in the Doy Mobile Home Park and then after maybe five years getting a house out here somewhere close to his mama's house so he can help out and I'll have some company.

We talk about having babies, too, but maybe I better skip that part with you, Mama. I *will* say that my very first girl will be named after you, Harriet Elizabeth Armstrong.

I just like doing stuff with him, Mama. We'll go over to the armory if there's a car show in town and get a couple chili dogs and walk around looking. Or we'll go out to his big brother Harold's house and him and Harold will go out with their rifles looking to get a couple squirrels while me and Sharon set in the kitchen with the baby and I'll tell her whatever problems I'm having and she'll give me advice like we were sisters.

When I'm in the Buick with him, driving the roads

late of a night, I feel safer than anywhere in the world, Mama, and my chest gets so full of happiness that I have to take deep breaths to live through it. Do you know that feeling?

There's some *real* personal stuff I need to talk to you about sometime. I haven't figured out yet what to do. If his big brother Harold didn't put it in his head that boys have *got* to have it—you know—that they're different from girls and just can't live without it once they turn teenagers, well, we wouldn't have the arguments we do. There was a time when I thought *I* couldn't wait to have it, too, but lately I'm so tired of his got-to-have-it that I'm not so sure I ever want it, if it makes me feel as bad inside as this. *Are* boys different from girls, Mama? I mean, is there something wrong with me or something wrong with him? Nearly everybody I know is doing it with somebody and I'm wondering if there's any among them who's really not having that wonderful a time, but I'm afraid to ask for fear there really *is* something wrong with me and somebody'll know then.

I just thought it would be different, watching them movies all those years.

He didn't want me to be in the school musical this year, so I didn't try out. He said he wanted me to be home when he gets off work from the gas station, not up at the school with all those boys. (He never has trusted Jim Wickline since Jim said something about me in the locker room, and Jim is in all the plays and he knew Jim'd be trying out for this one.) So I just stocked up on boxed soup and brownie mixes and stayed home watching TV till nine. Or later. I hate that waiting, Mama.

I hear from Daddy out in California. He wants me to come out there and live, but I tell him I like it here with Aunt Vi and Uncle David. Aunt Vi and I like to talk about you. At first she wasn't sure if I could take it, but I *wanted* to talk, so we sit around and she'll tell me the trouble you two were always getting into. She misses you as much as me and every now and then she'll be gone of a Sunday morning and I'll know she's over to the cemetery visiting with you. I got this whole notebook full of these letters so I don't need to go as much as Aunt Vi. Seems I'm talking to you all the time in this notebook, and even though the letters are all one-way, sometimes I'll get this feeling you're listening to me writing and even answering as best you can because right in the middle of writing about something I'll get this big flash of knowing what to do about it, like my mama just gave me the answer.

You remember that time I wanted that new Journey album so bad, I was so in love with them, and all the stores in town sold out before I could get one so you had one shipped up that very night on the Greyhound out of Charleston? I never forgot that, waiting in the parking lot of the Greyhound station with you, in the dark, for my Journey album to come out of that humongous door just above the wheels. I never will forget that.

This boy—Charlie—he takes good care of me, Mama, and he doesn't run around or anything and I like his family so much. Is that love? I hope I find out for sure because we've already got a trailer picked out and he's counting on me to marry him once he gets hired on at Babcox after graduation. And maybe his acne'll clear up in a couple years.

I'll talk to you later, Ma. I love you a lot.

Crystal

Clematis

WHEN Joe died, Ruth cut down the clematis vine growing up the trellis on the east side of her porch. She'd lived alone in the house for many years before Joe came to stay, and in all those years the clematis had never once bloomed. Its leaves had come out each spring, the thin brown vines growing firm and full of pulp, but no flowers had ever blossomed. Then Joe came, and when he spent his first night in her bed, she found the next morning two huge, lush purple flowers leaning out from the vines of her east porch trellis and she figured then that God was involved somehow and she married Joe.

She was sixty-seven when she married him and sixty-eight when he died. She wasn't sure she could

generate clematis flowers on her own, so she stripped
the trellis of its vines to avoid finding out and then
she took time for her sadness.

Love at sixty-seven is not much different from love
at seventeen. It is perhaps closer to the feelings of first
love than any time of romance in the years intervening
because at sixty-seven, as at seventeen, one is able to
live wholly for love and to believe it will last the rest
of one's life.

Ruth had never had much success with men before
Joe, anyhow. She had been twice married as a young
woman and though at the time she was much embarrassed when her second marriage fell through, for she
had been brought up by people who took great stock
in sticking with something once you've started it, in
her later years Ruth took a kind of delight in the fact
that she'd had more husbands than most women she
knew. When her young nieces asked her what kind of
a wedding she'd had, she'd cackle and ask which one,
the tall one or the short one (her two husbands had
varied greatly in height, and she loved referring to

anything having to do with them as the tall or the short: the tall honeymoon, the short wedding ring, the tall divorce, and so forth). She had a sense, even, that she was somehow sexier than other women her age because she'd been "heated and reheated," as she loved to describe it with a loud hoot.

At sixty-seven Ruth had been without a man in her life for twenty-two years, and she was as surprised and pleased to fall in love with Joe as a young girl is to be asked to the prom when she hasn't any notion at all of being asked, hasn't even thought about a dress.

Joe was fifteen years younger than Ruth, and this fact as well filled her with the greatest glee. Joe did not even qualify for the 10 percent senior citizen discount at Thompson's Drugs and Hank's Homemade Ice Cream Store, and she would watch him pay for a bottle of Sine-Aid or a coffee ice-cream soda and marvel that someone still paying list had fallen in love with her. And madly, at that.

Ruth met Joe in a poetry class at the Continuing Ed Center. From the first night she decided to make a good impression, because in addition to having the loveliest hands she'd ever seen on a man, Joe was also the class instructor. Ruth had signed up for the class because her friend Grace told her she could use her senior citizen discount, but after the first night, listening to Joe reading Walt Whitman aloud, she knew deep in her heart that for this she would have paid full price with a flourish.

Joe later told Ruth what it was about her that made him tremble, even that first night of class when he delivered the introductory lecture he could recite in his sleep.

"It was the braid down your back," he told her.

Ruth's gray hair was long, nearly to her waist, and she wore it in a long braid. When she was a little girl she'd worn her hair like this, and now again as an older woman. All the years in between she'd had it cut and curled at the beauty shop.

"And you did this wonderful little thing with your mouth," he said.

Ruth tried to get him to show her what the wonderful little thing was. At first they'd stood together in front of the bathroom mirror and Ruth had moved her mouth in as many ways as she could think how, hoping to reproduce the wonderful little thing, but Joe would keep shaking his head, saying, "No, that's not it. No, nor that." When this failed, she had him watch her with great vigilance throughout the day, instructing him to let her know the instant he saw the wonderful little thing so she might freeze it and run to the mirror for a look. But each time he saw it, he was so pleased to look at her that he forgot to say anything and by the time he thought of it, the wonderful little thing had disappeared like a flash of brilliant lightning.

Joe did not ask Ruth to dinner or to coffee or even to walk together to their cars in the parking lot until the last evening of the poetry class was done and her final paper was returned to her and he was no longer her instructor. Then he asked of her all three. She accepted as easily as he asked, and they went together to a quiet Chinese restaurant and talked until its closing hour, which was midnight. Joe went home with Ruth

and the purple clematis bloomed overnight, and, believing she would love him forever, Ruth asked Joe to
marry her and six days later he did. He moved in on
the seventh day and died three hundred and thirty-
nine days later of a heart attack as he lay sleeping on
a hammock in the back yard with a copy of *Leaves of
Grass* folded like a prayer over his chest.

What Ruth missed about Joe was the way he was
seized with an urge to cook late at night, and at eleven-
thirty the pots on the stove would be steaming and
Joe's face would be moist and pink as he shook out
spices with the abandon of a child, and at midnight
the two of them would be talking over great heaping
plates of some dish Joe had no name for, and their
talk would begin with questions: "What was one of
the happiest times you ever had?" "What was the
saddest thing that ever happened to you?" "What do
you want to do before you die that you haven't done
yet?"

And Ruth missed Joe's hands on her at daybreak.
He often woke at dawn and turned to her and lifted

open or off whatever she had on so he might put his lips against her skin and run his hands along the side of her body, just under the breasts and around the ribs, and settle his head on her heart to hear its beating. These times they were silent, as he woke her little by little, like a purple morning flower, and sometimes they made love or they simply slept again.

For many months after Joe died, Ruth had to run her own hands over her body at daybreak, so she might feel she still belonged to the world. And it was more months still that she pulled out the heavy pots beneath her kitchen cabinets and cooked her way across the thread of one day into another. And when she finally believed she would be able to live without Joe, she used her discount to sign up for a ceramics class at the Continuing Ed Center. If ever someone in her class asked her if she was married, or had ever been married, she would smile and, with a voice warm like the breath of a lover, answer, "Yes. Once. He died."

On the Brink

DON'T tell me that a guy can't be in love with two girls at the same time because that's exactly the predicament I'm in and I can remember when I didn't even like girls.

I play football and for some people that's an automatic sign that I'm a woman-chaser but I promise you I never was the type and I'm still not. I wanted to be a doctor when I grew up. My hero was Albert Schweitzer, for God's sake! I had no intention whatever of finding trouble with women. But that's exactly the trouble I'm in, and at eighteen no less.

One of the girls, she's been my neighbor since fourth grade. She's a couple years younger than me, just a sophomore, and I know that girl like I know myself.

I know every crush she's had since she was ten, including the one on me which started up about a month ago. Maybe my getting picked quarterback had something to do with it, I don't know. All I know is we ought to be out in her backyard this very minute in our shorts, throwing a Frisbee, instead of me sitting here and her sitting there with this terrible feeling in our chests and too afraid to talk about it.

Hell, I guess I've always loved her but when did I ever love her like *in* love? Not any time I can think of. There was that one Christmas when she got the cello and she came running over to our house—it was about seven in the morning; I was sixteen so she must have been fourteen—and she rang the bell but came busting through before anybody got to the door, and that morning, that moment, seeing her with her black hair all wild, wearing a robe full of big red hearts, and some Snoopy slippers, lugging that cello under her arm . . . She was like a stranger right then and I couldn't think of anything to say, could only stare at her, my mouth gone dry, and later when she came back over wearing regular clothes and her hair all combed, it was like it never happened, but I remembered it *did* happen, and when she left that note in my mailbox a couple weeks ago, I couldn't help thinking about that Christmas morning.

Her name is Mary Anne. I remember when she didn't even have any breasts, just these two little knobby points ruining the lines of her shirts. It was like they grew overnight, like pimples that sneak up on you while you're sleeping, and I noticed them all of a sudden the next day and I could hardly look in her direction when I spoke, I was so embarrassed to know she'd grown some overnight breasts.

After that I never really paid any attention to them, I swear to God, and it was only after the note in my box that I started thinking about them. Well, not *them*. Her. But in that way, you know. I mean, as a woman.

Which brings me to my second predicament, that being a real woman. A twenty-two-year-old woman in my karate class who's gone over the deep end for me. Now, she's got breasts which I noticed right away but that doesn't necessarily mean I love her more than Mary Anne. It just means she got to me and that made her special in a different sense.

Twenty-two. I can't believe it. She couldn't believe I was a high-school quarterback when I told her. Her eyes got big and she grinned real wide—she's got the best teeth of anyone I've ever met—and she said, "You're kidding." Well, right then I wished I was, wished I'd gone past eighteen and high school and senior prom straight into my twenties so I could pick up and *do* something when I meet a woman like this in karate class. But like an idiot I told her no, I wasn't kidding, and that she didn't look her age either, which I think she understood because she said thank you.

I want them both. God, I am a louse. But it's true. I want Mary Anne because she's familiar like an old stuffed animal, like that old calico dog I used to sleep with when I was a kid, and with her nothing would change, my life would be just this way, with her running over from next door every day and maybe we'd go to college together and get apartments side by side and everything would feel just right, the way things are when you can depend on them. And if I was lucky maybe I'd see her one more Christmas morning, maybe a lot of Christmas mornings, with her hair all wild and that robe and that look about her that stunned me into silence.

And I want the karate woman, Janice, because she scares the hell out of me and I wouldn't know what to expect from one minute to the other and I'd be like a spaceman cut adrift, lost in the galaxy, nothing to stand on or hold onto and all I could do was watch and wait to see what those good teeth would think of next.

The truth is, being eighteen and on the brink of everything just isn't what I thought it would be because there's two guys in me. One guy's married to a Kool-Aid mom, driving a Dodge Caravan full of kids to the Presbyterian church every Sunday. The other guy hasn't bathed in several days because he's too busy tooling all over the country on a chopper, picking up babes.

Maybe being in love is really just a way of not having to choose between lives. Maybe it's a way of having somebody else guarantee you'll never change and what you're really in love with is the rescue, being saved from the maniac you could be. Maybe you love people because they have this idea about you that's better than anything you could have cooked up on your own.

I'm in love with Mary Anne because she thinks I'm safe, and I want to be, I really do. And I'm in love with Janice because she thinks I'm not and I am so damned grateful for that possibility.

I guess I'll go find Mary Anne now and see what happens. Maybe if I mess up her hair before we talk, things will get clear.

A Couple of Kooks

We've bought a lot of things
To keep you warm and dry
And a funny old crib
On which the paint won't dry.
I've bought you a pair of shoes,
A trumpet you can blow,
And a book of rules
Of what to say to people
When they pick on you.
'Cause if you stay with us
You're gonna be pretty kooky, too. . . .

"Kooks"
DAVID BOWIE
The *Hunky Dory* album

THEY hadn't meant it to happen. Suzy and Dennis were such careful people in so many important ways. They flossed. They wore their seatbelts. Both gave up drinking when three of their good friends went away to Detox in the same month. He took vitamin C, she took iron.

So when this pregnancy did happen to these careful people, when Suzy confronted Dennis in the lobby of the free clinic with hot tears of distress running down her face, each was so shaken that for several days after, neither could be careful about anything and they came as near to hating each other as ever they had. They regretted everything—particularly the other's existence—and they prayed with all their hearts for miracles and redemption. They made promises. They wished for anything except that which was happening to them.

But, finally, the hate was exhausted, the prayers spent, and there was nothing left but to love each other again and compare. Suzy and Dennis always had compared everything. They had found that rather than try to describe an experience, it was easier to compare it to something else, something concrete, something they had both seen or heard or touched before. They drove to Towner's Woods to sit on top of a picnic table and compare this revelation from the free clinic.

Suzy said it was like the time they took that country road neither of them ever had been on, and they saw the garden full of sunflowers. She had thought the flowers were plastic, that something which looked like that could not be real.

Dennis said it felt like the night they were waiting for the lunar eclipse out on Johnson Road and a little plane had crossed the front of the moon, casting a shadow across its white face like a scene from a Spielberg movie.

They watched the squirrels and the blackbirds of Towner's Woods and they talked. They talked about telling their parents, they talked about telling Suzy's priest, and, eventually, they talked about giving away a baby like a little tree on Arbor Day. At sixteen there were only two real choices, but because Suzy believed most sincerely in a purgatory which harbored the souls of poor decision-makers, their choices became just one: to have a child and to give it away all in a breath.

They cried awhile, then they drove back and told their parents, who, after a few days of standing transfixed before open refrigerators, took it well. Suzy's priest also took it well and assured her she wouldn't be a shoo-in to purgatory.

Then while an attorney and a social worker searched for the man and woman who one day would walk this experience of sunflowers and Spielberg movies to its first day of kindergarten, Suzy and Dennis started thinking about time and Zippy the Pinhead.

Dennis had read in a book that a baby in the womb can hear everything on the outside—music, the purr of a cat, rain. He brought the book to Suzy who, with one hand resting quietly on her stomach, read with interest the page about the fetus being able to hear.

And the first thing they gave it was Zippy the Pinhead. One night in her second month, Dennis curled next to Suzy on her bed and opened a comic book.

"No matter who its parents are, you know they'll never read it Zippy," he said to Suzy.

He put his face near her stomach and began to read:

" 'I'm glad I remembered to Xerox all my undershirts,' said Zippy."

Like too much water, a giggle spurted from Suzy's mouth.

" 'Why is there a waffle in my pajama pocket?' "

Their parenting had begun.

Suzy and Dennis made lists of the people who were important to them, people sacred, people of such value that one generation has no choice but to pass them on to the next: Pee Wee Herman, Curly Howard, John Lennon.

Dennis talked above Suzy's stomach about Albert Einstein one day:

"Einstein said, 'Imagination is more important than Knowledge.' Remember that. It'll help when you flunk math quizzes."

They played their favorite music for the baby—*The White Album*, *Ziggy Stardust*—and one night they played their favorite creatures.

Whales.

Dennis showed up at Suzy's house with his Walkman and a cassette of humpback whale songs, and while Suzy lay on the couch, he stretched the headphones across her stomach.

"Wow," he said. "You're getting big."

He started the tape, spread himself out on the floor, and, holding Suzy's hand, fell asleep. Suzy slept, too, and the whales emptied their songs into her body.

"The baby will think it came from the sea," Suzy said later, when they woke up.

Dennis rubbed his eyes.

"It did."

They took it to the movies. After watching *Wings of Desire*, they sat on a park bench with ice-cream cones and talked to the baby about listening for angels—angels who would always be with it—and to watch for them, to watch for the quick shadows that are wings flying past the corner of the eye. Dennis told the baby never to worry, that it would never fall too far or too hard, because the angels would bear it up and keep it safe.

"And one of them might even be John Lennon," he added hopefully.

They watched *It's a Wonderful Life* on video, and they told the baby afterward that to be like George Bailey would be a good thing—to help in small ways, to be honest, to believe in miracles. Suzy told it about her own miracle, about the time her cat disappeared and was gone for weeks. Suzy's parents believed the cat was dead and gave up on it. But Suzy wouldn't. She told the baby about cutting a big star out of foil and hanging it in her window one night, believing it would lead the cat home like the Star of Bethlehem. And the next morning, Suzy told the baby, her cat was at the kitchen door.

In the fourth month Suzy told Dennis that the baby

was blowing bubbles, that she could feel them floating and popping against the walls of her uterus. And in the sixth month Dennis was resting his head on the hard mound Suzy's stomach had become, reading aloud *Krazy Kat*, when the baby rearranged itself. Dennis jumped so hard that he fell off the couch.

"What a woil'," he said to Suzy with a grin. "What a woil'."

They fed the baby their favorite foods: barbeques with slaw at Swenson's Drive-In; orange marshmallow peanuts; Moon Pies; fried bologna and mustard on Wonder bread; banana and mayonnaise sandwiches.

"It'll probably have these strange cravings all its life," Dennis told Suzy as they played miniature golf one afternoon. He fixed a stare into space:

" 'Gee, I'm hungry, but I just don't know what I want. Is it . . . is it . . . a *Moon Pie?*' "

Dennis told the baby to believe in God but not in religion. And to sing a lot. Suzy told it to feed the starlings, because nobody else does. And they both asked it to try to make friends with the Russians.

However, as the time for saying hello and good-bye

drew ever nearer, their lightness faded, and each began to feel a desperation, a sense of flailing, a tight anxiety much like that of a mother whose child is late coming home, who keeps looking out the window for sight of a small figure in a red coat. Suzy and Dennis began to realize how afraid they were, and that it was themselves the angels would have to bear up. It was they who must watch for the wings which might keep them from falling as they passed this child away from their own arms and into those of someone else who must keep it safe, must keep it warm, must be certain to watch long out the window for sight of a small figure in a red coat.

And it was finally in the last month, when the baby was large and awkward in Suzy's body, always trying to get comfortable in the womb it had outgrown, that both Suzy and Dennis understood that they needed to tell it of themselves. They had taught the baby their world. Now they must teach the baby its parents.

They drove back to Towner's Woods, to their favorite spot near the pavilion that looked out over sloping hills and small trees. The sun was warm this day. It was October and the baby would leave them before the month was gone.

Dennis asked Suzy to go first. He wasn't sure how to do it.

Months ago Suzy had stopped feeling sixteen, and with the deep sigh of a wise old woman, she put a hand on her stomach and began.

"If anybody asked me today what's the most important thing in my life, I'd say it was you. Dennis next. And I guess that's as good a family as anybody could want, so I hope you're not too disappointed in us.

"Some other mother's going to be raising you so you've got to pay attention to me now. We don't have much time left. I have to tell you about me because you'll grow up and maybe you'll feel these things you don't understand, or maybe you'll really like giraffes and you won't know why, and if you know deep inside it's because of me, it's because Suzy had those feelings or Suzy really liked giraffes, then you'll rest easier. You'll know it's just your mother in you.

"What I want to tell you about me, first, is that I love you very, very much."

She stopped, her eyes wet. Dennis reached out but she brushed him away, and, taking a strong breath, began again.

"And I'd keep you if I could but I truly can't. We don't have money or a place of our own. I don't know about anything except how to get through Physics with a C — and what days are good for hot lunch. I can't keep you. I can't."

Her eyes followed a cardinal in the trees.

"When I was a little girl I had a dollhouse and it had the prettiest things in it: a little flowered couch, a round white bathtub with feet, a shiny black telephone, a canopy bed in the big bedroom, and a little white crib in the little bedroom.

"It had a mom and a dad. But it didn't have a baby for the little white crib. Because I lost the baby that Christmas I got the dollhouse. I was only five or six, and I loved the baby best of all. All Christmas day I put it in and out of its little bed. There was a tiny piece of flannel in the bed, to keep it warm.

"But people came over for dinner, and they had kids, and the kids played with my things, and at bedtime that night I couldn't find the baby to put it in its crib.

"I cried and I cried and my parents searched through all the bags of wrapping paper and behind the tree and under the furniture. But they didn't find the baby.

"They tried to buy me a new one, but I never could find another baby just like the one I lost. So I left the crib empty. And I always worried about that baby. Where it had gone off to. Who it was with. Whether it needed that little piece of flannel lying in its crib.

"I know I'll worry about you that way. I guess there's no way to help that. But you'll be OK. You'll be better than OK. You'll be great."

Suzy stopped to untie her shoes. Her ankles were swollen with the fluid her body seemed to hoard this final month.

"I'll tell you some things about me. I don't drive a car because I'm afraid to try. Everybody but me has their driver's license now, and I'm pretty embarrassed. I still like coloring in coloring books. When I was fourteen I dyed my hair red one night and my parents made me get it stripped and permed and I looked like a Kewpie doll for weeks.

"When I was eleven I was so crazy about John Cougar Mellencamp that I spray-painted his name on the back side of our garage and my folks grounded me for two months.

"I love gray cats. I want to learn how to play acoustic guitar and sing like Tracy Chapman. And I'm scared to death of crows for some reason. But don't you be, it's silly. I think crows are the only thing I'm scared of.

"Someday I'd like to be a newspaper reporter. And I'd like to have ten cats living in my house with me. I want to go to Holland to see all the tulips and the windmills. And I really want to meet God someday."

She stopped, and Dennis waited while she searched her thoughts for the words that were important, the ones she couldn't risk forgetting.

"I'm really sorry I wasn't too thrilled when I found out about you. I hope you understand. When a person's sixteen and pregnant she just doesn't belong anywhere. I can't hang out with my old crowd anymore. Partly because of them (pregnant people give teenagers the jitters), and partly because of me, because I just can't get excited about a football game when I'm wondering whether you and I are going to survive everything.

"I can't hang out with the women who are old enough to have babies. They don't want me and I know I'm too dull for them.

"I was just scared I couldn't handle it. But I have handled it and I swear to God I don't regret a thing. I really don't. You're going to grow up and be better than I ever was. I know it. And you're going to change every single person you meet. You're going to make *everybody* better, the way you've made me and Dennis better before you've even gotten out of here.

"Everything's going to work for you, I know it. And from wherever I am, all my life I'll be sending you angels to hold you up. I promise."

Suzy took a deep breath then, and smiled at Dennis, who had been staring at the ground the whole time.

They sat in silence for several minutes. Then Suzy said with a whisper, "Your turn."

Dennis shook his head.

"I can't."

"What?"

"What you said—I can't do that good. I thought I had some words to tell it, but I lost them all listening to you."

He looked at her.

"I never knew that about your cat. Or that doll-house."

Suzy smiled and shrugged.

"Funny, the things you remember," she said.

She took Dennis's hand.

"Just talk to it like you talk to me. And give it some secrets to take with it. You can do it. You tell me stories all the time."

Dennis shook his head in doubt. Then he looked down at Suzy's stomach and grinned.

"You think I should tell it about the Fisher-Price schoolteacher?"

Suzy grinned back.

"Absolutely."

Dennis leaned over and tapped her stomach with his finger.

"Hey little dude. Heads up. It's me this time.

"OK, here's a Daddy-Dennis story you probably won't believe, but I'm going to tell you anyway. When I was six I fell madly in love with the Fisher-Price schoolteacher. She was only a couple inches tall, and hard as a rock, but I thought she was the most beautiful woman in the world. Every night I'd pull her out of my Fisher-Price schoolhouse and I'd sit her beside my bed and we'd just smile at each other."

Dennis looked at Suzy.

"That's why I love your mom. She has the same sweet little face. No kidding. She smiles all the time. You'd fall in love with her, too, if you saw her."

He reached out and touched Suzy's hair, then his eyes narrowed with thought as he looked toward the trees.

"My favorite place when I was a kid was my toy

box. I used to crawl inside it and close the lid and sit there in the dark. We've got a small house, and with two brothers, I couldn't find a place for myself. So I got in the box. I'd just sit there and think. I think a lot. It's my favorite thing to do besides listening to tapes. It's caused me enough hassles at school, believe me. But I can't seem to help it. My mind just gets up and goes off somewhere else."

He stopped. He thought hard for several seconds.

"There's not much I'm afraid of. Bats (even though Suzy says they're nice). Freddy Krueger movies. I can't sit through Freddy Krueger and don't you even try.

"I wish I'd been a teenager in the sixties because I'd have been so perfect for them. I'm a hippie in my heart but there's no place to be one right now. Everybody at school's into money and how long it'll take them to own their first BMW. I'd love an apple-red pickup, myself.

"Anyway, the sixties. I'd have loved to protest a war or sit in for integration. I'd have worn those psychedelic shirts and beads. And I bet if it was the sixties now, Suzy and I could find a way to keep you. We'd just go to some commune down the road and live. We'd grow our own beans and I'd learn to build things—chairs, maybe even houses.

"So if you ever get this urge to, like, join up with some group that's still wearing bell-bottoms and listening to The Doors, I figure you'll know where *that* came from.

"Suzy and me, we're just a couple of kooks. We're the only two people I know who can come out here and stare at the trees for two solid hours without saying a word. Maybe that's why I never liked school much. You're always having to talk.

"The best parts of me are the crazy parts and if you get those, you'll have all the good I've got. Like, I love sneaking out on rainy nights and walking naked in the backyard. I have seriously wondered at times if I wouldn't be better off in a nudist colony. If you get that part of me, I figure it's a pretty OK thing.

"I'd love to work in animation someday. I love old cartoons like the original Popeye, and Bosko, and 'Steamboat Willie.' Most animation today sucks out loud. I sure hope your . . . your . . . the people who raise you have sense enough to make sure you see the good stuff.

"Know what I wanted for Christmas last year? Chairry from Pee Wee's Playhouse and a talking Ed Grimley doll."

Dennis laughed.

" 'I'm going completely mental, I must say.' "

He rubbed Suzy's stomach.

"You really will be all right, kid. Suzy's sending angels. And I'll send money."

He laughed again.

When it was time to go, when both Suzy and Dennis knew that chances were this would be the last time they talked to their baby in Towner's Woods, they walked to the edge of a hill and looked out at Lake Rockwell, lying still and brown below them.

"Feels like rain," Dennis said quietly.

Suzy looked up at the sky.

"Good," she answered. "It'll like that."

And just as they turned to go, the sound of wings passed through the trees.